Where Are You, Little Frog?

Kayleigh Rhatigan

Illustrated by
Alik Arzoumanian

LARK
BOOKS
A Division of
Sterling Publishing Co., Inc.
New York / London

A cat chasing a mouse
is having lots of fun.

Can you guess where you are, little frog?

A dog doing his job,
is panting from the run.

Can you guess where you are, little frog?

A floppy hat on a head—
this is your third clue.

Can you guess where
you are, little frog?

A straw-filled little coop.
Someone lives here, but who?

Can you guess where you are, little frog?

Here's a patch of mud,
where big pink animals play.

Can you guess where
you are, little frog?

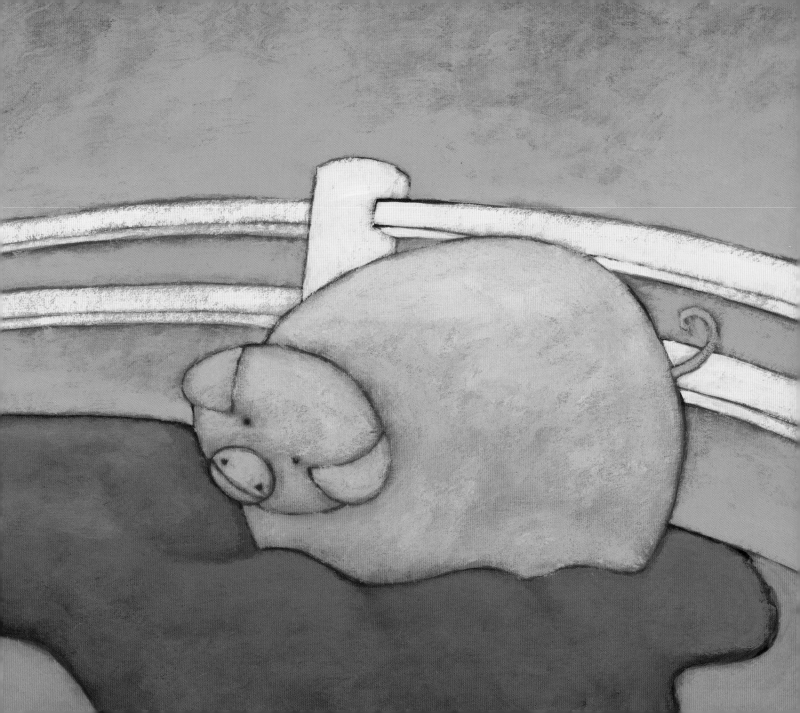

See the sleepy cow,
eating grass and hay.

Can you guess where you are, little frog?

There's a big red building
with X's on the door.

Can you guess where you are, little frog?

Inside a man sits down
with a bucket on the floor.

Can you guess where you are, little frog?

A very pointy pitchfork
leans against the wall.

Can you guess where you are, little frog?

A beautiful white horse stands very tall.

This is your final clue!
Where are you, little frog?

For Lara & Nina, my little cousins
–KR

For Hovan
–AZ

Rhatigan, Kayleigh, 1997-
  Where are you, little frog? / Kayleigh Rhatigan. -- 1st ed.
    p. cm.
  ISBN-13: 978-1-60059-348-2 (alk. paper)
  ISBN-10: 1-60059-348-8 (alk. paper)
  I. Title.
  PS3618.H44W48 2008
  811'.6--dc22

                            2007052135

10 9 8 7 6 5 4 3 2 1

First Edition

Published by Lark Books,
A Division of Sterling Publishing Co., Inc.

387 Park Avenue South, New York, NY 10016
Text © 2008, Kayleigh Rhatigan
Illustrations © 2008, Alik Arzoumanian

Distributed in Canada by Sterling Publishing,
c/o Canadian Manda Group, 165 Dufferin Street
Toronto, Ontario, Canada M6K 3H6

Distributed in the United Kingdom by GMC Distribution Services,
Castle Place, 166 High Street, Lewes, East Sussex, England BN7 1XU

Distributed in Australia by Capricorn Link (Australia) Pty Ltd.,
P.O. Box 704, Windsor, NSW 2756 Australia

If you have questions or comments about this book, please contact:

Lark Books
67 Broadway
Asheville, NC 28801
828-253-0467

Manufactured in China

ISBN 13: 978-1-60059-348-2

For information about custom editions, special sales, premium and corporate purchases, please contact
Sterling Special Sales Department at 800-805-5489 or specialsales@sterlingpub.com